K. A. Zartman

I0526603

Lavender Moon

Lavender Moon Publishing

Lavender Moon Publishing

ISBN: 978-0-578-22909-6

PRINTED IN THE UNITED STATES OF AMERICA

Table of Contents

CHAPTER 1

THE BUZZER AT the front door sounds. I glance up to see customers and continue to enjoy the feel of my partner's fingers as they push in and out of my vagina. Thirty minutes to closing, and I can bend over and feel him inside me.

We are standing in the office behind a high counter to avoid detection. There have been many times discovery has halted his fingers or my mouth on his cock. Perhaps rude behavior—however, we take advantage of every moment, as he is married, and our affair is secret.

Locking the front door and shutting off the rows of fluorescent lights, we move to the mattress department, and I pull him onto me and pull down his pants and boxers. Grabbing his erection, I pull him to me and spit on my hand to transfer the wetness to my vagina. Bending over, I am now ready for some strong thrusts, though over too quickly.

Mark's age of fifty-two affects his stamina. We have tried various methods to prolong his orgasm, none of which were successful. Our twenty-five-year affair has brought many pleasures. I often think of events that lead down the road of sexual satisfaction in older people. I'm sure my kids could not imagine their mom having wonderful, illicit sex in the store, hotels, and the front seat of our Ford delivery pickup.

We are driving to Half Moon Bay, playing with each other after a busy day at the San Francisco Furniture Market. He pulls me off his cock, threatening to come, and slows to the shoulder. Mark wants me and quickly shoves his fingers into my wetness. I am so aroused and cannot wait for him to pull his pants to his knees and take me. The pickup has a roomy front seat. No console, just what we need for comfort. Over soon, it is quite late, so we head home to sleep some before our day begins again at 8:00 a.m.

Another long day at Market, and we have been invited to dinner and drinks. We head to the Caribbean Zone, a bar set in a Doobie

Brother's airplane in a restaurant in downtown San Francisco. I am on my second Long Island Iced Tea; Mark is on his third. Guess I will drive us home. We had planned to go straight home, though the drinks have amped our arousal, so I pull into our favorite hotel and register us.

Sharing the small shower, we get clean and hurry to pull down the comforter and start to play. As he circles his fingers in me with one hand and teases my clitoris with the other, I start to wiggle and find I am not paying attention to him; he is hard and panting, but I want to delay this. We have been in the ninety-dollar room only half an hour—the cost of illicit sex not just in dollars.

CHAPTER **2**

HOLIDAYS ARE THE worst. Sometimes the kids are with me, sometimes with my ex, and never with Mark. I become familiar with small turkey breasts, instant potatoes, and a yummy dessert to soothe the spirit. It is usually a day of recriminations but not realizations—hard to imagine any future changes.

Afternoon naps, and I am in a better mood. Life is hard. Get up and get your clothes ready for tomorrow. Empty the dishwasher. There is always a better day to replace the bad one. I call Mom and Dad to wish them happy anniversary and listen to the ever-present health complaints and sibling rivalries. As the family black sheep, I am the only one not in Colorado close to parents, brothers, and sisters. My parents are blissfully unaware of my relationship with Mark, as are my siblings. All are married and have children that keep life exciting. My own kids do not disappoint as well. Three teen-agers with individual challenges, the oldest, soon to marry and start his own family. Am I ready to take on the title of Grandma? I refuse to dress in housecoats and have kinky permed hair, the typical appearance of my own grand-mothers, though I will send checks for birth-days and holidays, a grandparent tradition and favorite of the grandkids.

CHAPTER 3

MARK SURPRISES ME one morning at work. He presents me with a manila envelope. I can see the excitement in his face and eyes. Opening the envelope, I find two pornographic videos and a discount coupon to use on the next orders. We make plans for dinner and a movie night at my house. After we enjoy chicken stir-fry and a few beers, we settle in on my comfortable sofa and start the first video.

There is no buildup to the sex; a naked couple is pounding away in a squeaking lawn chair and making lots of noises. We both start to laugh and make disparaging comments regarding the budget of the film. The cameras move in closer, and genitals are visible; Mark and I kiss and begin to play with each other. The man in the film suddenly pulls out of the woman and comes on her stomach; the woman continues to moan and tries to coax the man hard again.

Bored with the film, we turn attention to each other. Mark aggressively puts fingers in me, and I pull him to my mouth and establish a fast rhythm. We are both breathing heavily, and I turn over, so he can take me from behind; a few more thrusts, and I hear him grunt, "I love you," and then come hard. The thought crosses my mind that the man always seems to get satisfied but not necessarily the woman. Will we ever be equal?

We wait another week to watch the second film. We order pizza and beer and start the second film. Much better than the first, it has an actual story line with no sex until the middle of it…two lovers in a sixty-nine position and moaning loudly. She is wet, and he is quite hard. Mark and I decide to duplicate the action on screen. The sofa is not large enough for us to get comfortable, so we both roll to the floor and continue our endeavors. Then we slowly make love and fall asleep on the living room rug. The film has ended, and Mark jumps up and pull on his clothes; he is panicked that his wife will be upset. I hate this disappearing act he frequents.

CHAPTER 4

IT HAS BEEN a long, tiring week at the store. Mark brings over Chinese food and says he has a couple hours while his wife is visiting friends. He has a surprise for me after we eat. The sweet-and-sour chicken is hot and delicious. We enjoy the meal, and sheepishly, he pulls out a manila envelope from his jacket.

"I thought we could have some fun."

The envelope holds a dildo. He pulls it out and says, "Get naked. I want to use this on you."

Smacking my ass, he says, "Hurry and bring some massage oil with you."

When I return, he pushes me to the bed and jerks my legs apart. Squirting oil on me, he begins to rouse my clitoris. Once he sees me wiggling, he thrusts the dildo in me and aggressively pulls it in and out.

I tell him, "Easy, easy, be a little gentler."

He stops and says, "Sorry, I got carried away."

"Yes, you did. I would rather have the real thing."

Disappointed, Mark says okay and complies with my demands.

I feel bereft after Mark leaves. Am I just his for sex? Yes, I guess I am.

Mark is quiet the next morning. He gives me a hug and kiss and says, "I'm sorry. I don't know what came over me. I was just so excited."

We have a quiet week, no sex, each of us reflecting on our relationship. Perhaps our feelings for each other have started to change. The end of the week proves it is not, as Mark grabs me and forces me to a mattress. He is all over me and repeats he loves me again and again. How can I resist? Twenty-five years of knowing each other and still no hope of a future? I contemplate, how did I end up here?

I have made mistakes before, two marriages, two divorces, both alcoholics, one the father of my three children. I need to ponder my situation.

My first husband, James, was a marine I met while going to school for the navy. A whirlwind relationship, and I was unaware of his drinking excesses and need for drugs.

Pregnant with my second son, I recall a beach picnic in Hawaii. It is a barbeque, and James dumps the hot coals from the Weber close by in the sand of a Waikiki beach. Ready to leave, I walk through the hot coals, and screaming I run into the ocean and then collapse out on the beach. James runs to pick me up, though at eight months pregnant, I am too heavy for him. Both feet and my legs are severely burned and blistered from the coals and liquified sand. He procures some help to get me to the car, and we head home to his apartment in Waikiki. In pain, I ask him to take me to the emergency room at Tripler Hospital. He refuses.

I crawl to the door of the apartment, and James brings me a bucket of cold water for relief of the pain. It helps to ease me through the night, though in the early-morning hours, I look at my feet and legs, raw, red, hamburger. I need the hospital, and James finally agrees. The doctor debrides the surface skin, a very painful process, and tells me to come back every day for more debridement of the tissue.

James is not happy but will comply with the orders. He can be such an asshole at times.

Just a few painful weeks after the burns, I go into labor with my second son. He is a footling breach, and the doctor, familiar with combat wounds but a neophyte with complicated births, tries to turn him before the birth. Thirty-six hours and no luck turning him. His heart rate and breathing are too low. The doctors decide to use forceps to pull him from me. God, what an awful experience! Nothing like my first son's birth.

When they bring the baby to me, I am shocked to see the angry bruises on his face and shoulders. More concerning is the huge hematoma on the crown of his head. The doctors reassure me it will dissipate with time, but he must wear protective headgear until it disappears.

James has been absent at the hospital on duty at the airfield.

Another memory surfaces.

James in working on a carburetor in the kitchen. He has been drinking and argues over the meal I am cooking. Pissed off, he suddenly throws the carburetor at me just as I open the refrigerator door. The door bears a large dent and hole with eggs and salad dressing leaking on the floor. Thankfully the neighbor has heard the shouting and comes over to restrain James and calls the MPs for assistance.

James was a violent man, and I put up with him for ten years. Am I making another mistake with Mark? He is not violent, just needy. I realize I missed the warning signs with both husbands, and I don't want another error to change my life again.

CHAPTER 5

AN OPPORTUNITY ARISES for Mark and me to go to a furniture show in Reno. Mark and I will be able to spend the night, a first. I am excited.

At the end of the first day, we spend a few hours in the casino: free drinks and we win a little money. It is after midnight when we return to the room; we are both tired. So, we take a quick shower and, wrapped in towels, fall asleep next to each other. So much for romance when you are older.

Mark wakes with an erection, and we have quiet sex while waiting for our room service breakfast. We talk about our relationship and the future. He is unwilling to divorce, and I see no future ahead. I begin to think about retirement and ending our affair. Love cannot overcome all obstacles, it seems.

I decide to end our affair and call our lawyer to figure out the details.

Decision finalized, I plan to move to Colorado where my parents and siblings live. Mom and Dad could use some help with daily living.

Accepting my new circumstances, I buy a new house: four bedrooms, three baths, and a large office. Room for Mom and Dad to move here when they are ready. I become restless. Twenty-five years of working and then nothing.

Driving to the grocery store, I notice an older home on a large corner lot, busy street, and considered commercial. I write down the phone number and call when I get home. I could open a small store, and the large lot will accommodate my dog, Lucy, in a fenced-in area.

I arrange to meet the listing agent and look at the property. A quick tour and I decide to lease the house. I return home and begin ordering inventory for the new business. The shop opens, and I fill it with gifts and furniture for women. The large lot holds gazebos, metal garden accents, and a fenced area for Lucy.

Relaxed and easy to manage, the shop does well. Frequent, middle-of-the-night phone calls from Mom and Dad prompt a move closer to them. I close the shop and look for another larger location. Anchored next to a large, well-known retailer, the new shop does well, though Mom's and Dad's health require more of my time.

Two years in the new shop, and I become quite ill. Fortunately, my son, Tony, can open and manage the shop. After four visits to an emergency room, I am finally admitted to the hospital: 105-degree temperature and a diagnosis of sepsis. I am in a coma, all of my organs are in failure, emergency surgery is scheduled, and my kids are notified Mom will not make it another twenty-four hours. Experimental antibiotics are tried, and I begin the road back. Three months in the hospital and enormous medical bills due to poor health insurance soon bring ruin to my life and 401k. Bankruptcy and losing the house are a certainty. Sixty years old, and I must start over. Several unsettled years pass—limited employment, rental house and further declines in Mom's and Dad's health.

Bathing, changing diapers, and many emergency visits now consume my life. No man to comfort me, I occasionally have the energy to pleasure myself. I yearn for a man again, but my life does not allow me time to find another.

CHAPTER **6**

I MOVE IN with Mom and Dad as they now require twenty-four-hour care. A few years pass, and Dad is failing fast; his normal weight of 225 pounds has dropped to 110 pounds, and he is a shadow of his former self. I reflect on his final days. Dad is restless. I change him and put him in his wheelchair; he can enjoy the full sunshine on the back porch. He has not eaten or drunk water for four days; his blood pressure is very low and his breathing slight.

Fearing today is his last, I call my brothers and sisters to come over. I administer a dose of morphine to calm him and help his breathing. Mom takes his hand, and I roll him toward her. She is anxious, knowing Dad is going, and begs him to fight. He opens his eyes, sighs, and takes a last labored breath. No pulse. Dad is gone. I call the hospice nurse to come over and pronounce Dad. Once she arrives and fills out the legal paperwork, I remove Dad's clothes and wet diaper. I wash him as tears fall and put him in a clean T-shirt and boxers.

It is Mom's wish to dress him in his WWII flight suit. My sister, Susan, helps me to dress him. The suit has a long zipper, and it is a struggle to bend his arms and legs and feed them through the openings. We finish dressing Dad and call the funeral home to come and take Dad. A short time later and the funeral home representative arrives and rolls in a gurney to place Dad on. He is laid in a black body bag, and we kiss him goodbye before the long zipper takes him from us. A sudden thought of C130s unloading the endless black bags arriving from Vietnam. The funeral home will return Dad's ashes and deliver the flag he has earned by dying. Another brave soldier being carried off the battlefield of life.

A few short years pass, and I repeat the process with Mom. She has refused food and drink; a raging fever causes her to shiver, and she is in pain from the gangrene of her feet. I stroke her hair and give her the morphine. She quiets and sits up to say, "Stay with me. I don't want to die alone." I call the family and tell them today is her last; everyone is out of town. I hold her hand and wait for the end. Her pulse is faltering, and finally I can feel it no more. I call to have her pronounced and then call the family. I dress her in her favorite Swiss pajamas and sit down to wait for another black body bag. How many children have the privilege to hold the hand of a parent as they pass? God, the singular events of life. It goes on!

CHAPTER 7

A GREAT CHANGE is needed; the stress of twenty-four-hour care has taken a toll. I need something else to keep me busy and add some income to my low bank balance. I apply for a job at a large, local furniture store. I am hired and ready to go back to work.

Looking over the available males, I am not enthusiastic about the choices. There is one not married and no girlfriend but thirty years younger than I am. I don't feel old, just needy for the comfort of a man. I entertain myself with dreams of the one man, tall, heavily muscled, and handsome. I frequently have daydreams of us fucking while I hold his firm ass. He is rather shy and inexperienced, so I teach him how to receive and give pleasure. Just dreams, but maybe someday.

Five years on the job, and I begin to feel lightheaded and try to stand—I wobble on my feet. One of the managers noticed my distress. I cannot talk—only garbled noises come out of my mouth. I have had a stroke; the hospital confirms and orders several tests as my heart is also irregular.

A month of rest at home and results of the tests confirm I need open-heart surgery. My aorta and root for it plus a large aneurism require replacement to keep me alive. My kids are once again informed Mom might not make it through the surgery.

The surgery is scheduled, and my daughter comes to help me set up my bills on autopay as it will be a long time until I can work again. I wake up two days after the surgery barely able to move and with large, angry incisions down my chest.

Four days after the surgery, I am returned to the operating room—the pericardial sack surrounding my heart has filled with blood and needs to be cut open to release the fluid. Several days pass, and I can see the additional scars. I wonder if a man can look past them and enjoy my large breasts.

I have now been in the ICU for three weeks; my lungs and kidneys have failed. Forced to have a very uncomfortable oxygen mask every day and night, my face bears the bruises form the tight straps.

CHAPTER 8

I GARNER COMPLIMENTS from the nursing staff because my hair is purple. I wanted a bit of fun before surgery. The noise and constant interruptions of a critical patient do not allow me to sleep for more than a half an hour at a time. I am miserable, a foreign feeling to me—when will this end?

Another interruption, I wake to two male nurses attempting to catheterize me. One is a student nurse listening to the other's instructions but unable to place the catheter. His fumbling arouses me, and soon a female nurse arrives to properly place the catheter. The males need further education but not on me.

My lungs continue to fail, and another surgery is planned. Can I take anymore setbacks? Yes, I am strong enough to survive everything I am subjected to. I have been in cardiac ICU for a month.

Slowly I can walk a little and go for various tests and procedures. I begin to see a glimmer of light through drowsy eyes. My hand frequently slips down to rub my genitals and quiet my nerves. Hospital gowns and no underwear offer the freedom. I have been ordered to go for cardiac rehab three times a week; it will be six to nine months before I can possibly go back to work.

Fortunately, I have a small 401k from the furniture store to live on for a few months. I show up for my first rehab session, and a muscled young man explains how it works and what is expected. He has placed a hand on me several times and ends the interview with a blood pressure reading. My hand is on his strong shoulder for support. I suddenly feel a spark of energy below my waist and think this could be interesting.

CHAPTER **9**

MY SECOND REHAB visit I start on the tread-mill, and Ben comes to give me instructions. He is staring at the angry, red incision visible on my chest. His hand brushes the scars and then glides down my breasts.

After ten minutes on the treadmill, I am a bit wobbly, and Ben comes over to steady me. I reach out for support and brush against his front. Feeling like teenagers, we flirt with each other. We continue our flirtation over the next few sessions and finally decide to get together.

I am twice his age, have wrinkled skin, red scars… What will he think when we get naked? Okay, lights out. We are having dinner before going to my house; a few glasses of wine to bol-ster my courage, and I scoot closer to him in the booth. We kiss briefly, and I begin to massage the front of his jeans. Ben responds and hardens

under my touch. He compliments me on my freshly dyed lavender-colored hair.

We sexually tease each other on the way to my house; we are both excited. We quickly move to the bedroom, and I fumble a bit with his jeans, a throwback style, all buttons and no zipper. I am pleased and excited to discover Ben is well endowed. I take him in my mouth and taste the tang of a man, forgotten for so many years. He reaches up and pulls my camisole over my head. I am braless since the incisions have not fully healed. He captures one of my breasts and massages the nipple to attention. Soft moans from both of us further our excitement. I tell him to play with me, and he seems to know what to do. He gently pulls me off him and asks if he should use a condom. I laugh and assure him I am too old to become pregnant. He also laughs and positions himself to take me. I wrap my legs around him and place my hands on his ass, pulling him to me. I tell Ben it has been fifteen years since I have had sex, and I am so glad to have the opportunity again. He beings to pant and thrust harder. All too soon, he climaxes inside me; casually playing with my breasts, he says, "I

can't believe I just had sex with a seventy-year-old woman, and I enjoyed it." I respond and tell him, "I can't believe I just had sex with a thirty-four-year-old and enjoyed it."

We talk softly and get to know each other a little. Glancing at my bedside clock, I suggest we have a shower and then drive back to his car. I get up and go into the bathroom and turn on the shower. Nice, warm water spills over me and Ben as he joins me. I grab the jasmine-scented body wash and start to massage it into Ben's shoulders. Smooth, strong, muscles ripple beneath my fingers, and I move down to feel the valleys between his belly muscles. Squeezing more soap, I seize his cock and hand the soap to him. He mimics my actions, and we are both foaming and clean. A sudden thought of my old body next to his strong, hard one. Fluffy white towels dry us, and Ben give me a quick kiss and says, "I enjoyed this."

CHAPTER **10**

THE NEXT SESSION gives me a second opportunity to see Ben. We both shyly smile and arrange to meet. We attack each other as soon as I open the door. We each are pulling clothes off as we head to the bedroom. Frantic to couple again, he pushes me over the side of my bed and forces his cock into me. A few moments, and he grunt and stills. Geez! Is it over already? I roll over and begin to gently fondle his cock, sticky from our earlier union. I get up and head to the bathroom; returning with a warm, soapy washcloth, I grab his flaccid cock and clean him up. Pushing the cloth between my legs, I clean myself as well. I return to the bed and pull him to my mouth; carefully, I draw him in and out, in and out, hoping to stimulate an erection. My upper denture slips from sucking, and I quickly remove it and continue. I clamp down harder and feel him jerk a bit. He

becomes hard and begins to play with me—finally I have his attention. Ben warns me he is going to come, so I back off. I am not ready for round two to end. I tell him to continue with his fingers, and soon I feel the pull and pulse of my orgasm building, so I wrap my legs around his hips and grab Ben's ass for support, pulling him into me. I come first, and he follows seconds later. We both relax and doze off.

Hours later I wake to Ben rolling me over, and he takes me quickly from behind. Am I supposed to have this much pleasure at my age? Yes, I deserve it! He playfully slaps my ass and says he would like to fuck it next time. Swallowing my anxiety, I tell him okay. Courage in the field.

I push the grocery cart down the aisle and try to remember the prep I did for a colonoscopy year back. I pick up the MiraLAX, magnesium, and then Gatorade. The next day I spend most of it in the bathroom and think of why I am here.

Ben arrives and asks if I am ready. "Yes, are you?" He nods and pushes me to the bedroom. Quickly we are naked, and he plays with me, working his hands to my ass. I reach over and

hand him a tube of lubricant. I am on my knees and feel him spread the lube on me, and him asking if I am okay, he slowly sinks into me and says it is so tight. "God this feels good. I have never done this before." I tell him to be gentle, and I am rewarded when he draws a few fingers over my clitoris. It is not long before he mumbles he is going to come. He grunts and collapses on me.

"Thank you; that was fun. I would like to do that again."

"Not today, Ben."

CHAPTER **11**

A FEW DAYS pass, and I am restless. Have I been taking advantage of Ben? Perhaps we are both adults and have consented to our behavior. Before our next meeting, I dye my hair, and the purple becomes a soft shade of lavender. Ben compliments me on my hair, and I draw him to the living room to talk.

"What do you think of our relationship? Where can it go?"

I am feeling uneasy with the age difference. He contemplates for a few minutes and tells me to relax.

"I am comfortable with you and enjoy our time together. You are overthinking this—don't worry."

Pulling me to him, he rips my camisole off me and kisses my scarred chest and draws his erection to me. He becomes aggressive and thrusts hard, telling me he loves this and me. I pull away from him and say, "No, you can't. I am too old. Please rationalize this. I am twice your age. I could die at any time; this is just sex, Ben."

We don't see each other for a week, and he is at my door.

"I thought about this all week. I am comfortable with our relationship. You please me more than my girlfriends have. I find you attractive, and now I would like to prove it to you."

I tell him, "Okay, but please don't get too attached to me. The age difference bothers me, even it if doesn't bother you."

The dilemma keeps me up at night. I need to end this, but not tonight. I pull Ben to me, and we have hard sex. Quietly, I talk to him, "Think about the future, Ben. I could die at any time, and you have forty or fifty more years. You need a girlfriend your own age to build a future." Shaking his head, he is adamant: "You are the one I want. Don't turn me away."

CHAPTER **12**

THE NEXT TIME Ben calls, I make an excuse, though I want him. We need to end this before he is damaged. I falter a few times, and dinner goes untouched on the stove. Ben does not understand my reluctance, but I think he is getting the message.

He calls me a few times, and I say no. Months go by, and I haven't heard from him. I do hope he has found someone to build a future with.

Now on my own, I am to continue rehab but in a local gym. The same equipment I am used to and lots of muscled males to judge. One named Andy, fifty something, has begun to flirt with me. He loves my hair and asks how I got the chest scars.

"Come, I'd like to take you to dinner."

We walk to a nearby restaurant and have spaghetti and a glass of wine. We flirt and get closer to a relationship. Andy is single, divorced, and at fifty-five, a virile example of what I need.

We arrange to meet at his house in a few days. Opening the door, Andy is in shorts, no shirt. Close up, he is a treat. We have a few drinks, and he start to massage my neck and shoulders as his hands begin to dip lower. He pulls my camisole off and looks over my scars. Kissing my chest, he says, "I want you." Pinching some extra flesh at my middle, he says next time in the gym, he will help me lose it. I laugh and tell him to continue. I pull his shorts down, no underwear, and he has an erection. I take him into my mouth and begin to suck. Andy returns the favor and circles a few fingers in me. After enjoying this for several minutes, he draws me to his bedroom.

Turning on some music and a ceiling fan, he says, "Let me come in you." "Go for it." He pumps and pumps. I am becoming a little tired and hope it will end soon. He tells me that steroids affect his ability. "Sorry, tell me if you want to stop." I lie and tell him to continue. I pull him tighter to me and apply pressure to his ass to encourage him. "Keep it up, baby. I am close." Exploding in me, he is panting and gulping for air. Smiling, he says, "Now it is your turn." Turning me over, he pulls my legs apart and begins to massage my sex, utilizing his ejaculate for moisture. I am much faster to climax, and soon we are both breathing heavy.

We agree to another session at my house after a workout at the gym. Needing a shower, we strip and start to massage and clean each other. Andy is anxious and suddenly draws me to him. "Pleasure me." I comply, and he forces me against the shower wall and takes me violently. Chuckling, he says, "That's the fastest I've come in years."

Slipping out of the shower, Andy is looking at me and says, "You are getting fitter. I like it." Andy dries me and draws us to the bed. Forcing my legs apart with his, he gently parts my pubic hair and clamps down my clitoris and inserts fingers into me. My climax is close, so I sit up and pull him onto his back; grabbing his erection, I sit on it and pursue a strong rhythm. Andy starts to groan and grabs my hips hard. Guiding us through, we soon climax loudly together. "Time for another shower," and he throws another towel at me. Was sex ever this exhausting when I was young?

I tell Andy I'm tired and hit the bed for twelve hours. Maybe I need to find a seventy-year-old with my same appetites. Do they exist?

Recharged after hours in the gym, Andy suggests we have a steak and return to his house. My hair is clean, shaved legs, and I'm ready for a fun night. We go to a local steakhouse, and fifteen minutes later, we are presented with steaming plates. The steak is a little overcooked, so I have trouble chewing it with my dentures. Andy notices my frustration and offers to order something easier for me to chew. Nice guy, just an old woman. Andy knocks over a water glass in his lap. A nearby waiter sees the problem and brings over a cloth towel. I start to soak up the excess water and feel Andy harden beneath my fingers. Check please! We head to his house.

He pulls my hand to the front of his jeans and pushes it down to his erection. He is hard and anxious; pulling his jeans to his ankles, he walks awkwardly toward the bedroom. He jeans restrict his movement, so he stops and tells me to sit on him. Lifting me up and down, up and down, the pressure of his hands will bruise my hips, though I do enjoy the bounces. Needing to change positions, I spin around, so my back is to Andy, and then he comes loudly. Andy notices the angry red marks on my hips and offers a massage. "Great, do you best." He has wonderful, strong fingers and sweet-smelling massage oil. I can't resist his hands, and my legs spread on their own, awaiting those magic hands.

I return home, have a hot shower, and notice my bruised hips and the need to color my hair. If I want to continue my sexual endeavors, I need to maintain my body and appearance. You can't always have the lights out. The following weekend, a holiday, Andy and I are enjoying barbequed ribs and beer in his neatly landscaped backyard. We have talked and enjoyed each other without sex all afternoon. The sun is setting, and we cuddle together on a spacious chaise lounge. Fondling each other, I roll to my side, and we spoon together, his hands sliding from my breasts to my ass. He gently runs his hand between my cheeks, and I tense in anticipation; he continues south, and

we make long, gentle sex, somewhat of a nov-
elty. Andy is subdued the next time in the gym.
Sheepishly, he hugs me and says he has met
someone else.

CHAPTER 13

OKAY, I'M NOT really upset as I have been observing another man for several weeks in the gym. Tall, muscled, and I think retired military, given his put-together appearance. His name is Sam, and we have flirted while using the weight bars. Sam helps me to progress to heavier weight and confirms that he is ex-military. A marine gunnery sergeant, two tours in Vietnam, purple heart from shrapnel wounds. I disclose I am ex-navy, aviation, an avionics tech for a base in Texas. We received hundreds of helicopters shot down in Vietnam. There is an endless supply for us to rob good parts from and send the copters back to Asia. Sam says he was saved several times by helicopters and crews shooting at the NVA. "Can we get together? I'd like to get to know you better." We decide to go to a nearby Subway and talk specifics about Nam.

I have a passion for tales of Vietnam. A war too long and with no clear winner, I add that I love war movies and the history of WWII. Sam says, "I can't believe it. A woman with my own interests!" We spend an hour or so chatting and agree to meet again at the gym. I am excited about our meeting only two days away. I clean the house and buy some liquor for easing our conversation.

After I meet Sam at the gym, we have an intense workout as he shows me some new machines and how to use them. We are both sweating and decide to go to my house for a shower and dinner in. I open the front door, and Sam sees my art studio. Admiring my paintings, he says, "You are quite a woman—purple hair and loves war." I take him into my library, and he sees my selection of movies. He pulls *Midway* from the shelf and says it is one of his favorites. Studying the back cover, he pulls me to him and kisses my cheek. "I'm a fan of Charlton Heston. Can we watch this tonight?" "Sure, I'll order some pizza after our shower."

I draw him to my bathroom, and he is wary of taking off his clothes. I tell him to relax. "We will be good together." I tug off my

camisole, and Sam startles. "What happened to you?" I explain about my open-heart surgery a few months ago. He nods and gives me a hug. I pull off my yoga pants and lacy gray underwear. He returns the favor and removes his jeans and no underwear. I put two fluffy white towels on hooks next to the shower and reach in to start the water. Waiting for the water to warm, Sam hugs me and says, "I may be a little rusty at this. It has been a while." Sam has been celibate for years. I kiss him and tell him that he is going to get lucky tonight. He smiles, and we step into the shower. We explore each other with soapy hands, and he soon has an erection. We rinse, and I tell Sam to stay in a towel. I don a robe—no free show for the pizza driver. I take his hand and lead him to the living room sofa. We drink a few beers, waiting for the pizza, and fondle a bit. He plays with my breast, and I pull his towel up to expose him to me. I gently suck, and he says, "Whoa! Take it easy, or I won't last long." "Just getting to know you better, Sam. Relax and enjoy."

Pizza is here, and we talk about *Midway*, which I will start after our meal. I turn on the

Blu-ray, and the film begins. We watch for a while and begin to fondle. Sam pats my thigh and wants to watch the film… We have all night. Nodding to his wish, we settle in till the credits roll, and I guide him to the bedroom. His rather rough hands are all over me and in me. I stroke his erection and guide him to me. This is going to be a quick fuck. Sam pants and moments later explodes.

"Sorry, but it has been years since I had sex."
"The dry spell is over, Sam."

I clean both of us and begin to coax Sam again with my mouth. Yes, we are going to be good together. Sam is hungry, and we hump again, desperate for satisfaction. We talk in the aftermath, and I learn that Sam is a single, sixty-six years old, a retired Marine gunnery sergeant. Never married, no kids or family. I, on the other hand, seventy-one, three kids, eight grandkids, one great-grandchild, and very ready for a man like Sam. "What other movies do you have?" I take his hand and lead him back to the library. *In Harm's Way*, a John Wayne, Kirk Douglas film, and personal favorite. *Tora, Tora, Tora*, *Patton*, *The Enemy Below*, *Das Boot*, and a few others. Sam says, "I'll be over every weekend."

I smile and say, "I look forward to it." "Semper Fi, gunny; see you in the gym!"

A quick workout in the gym, and we go to my house. Sam is shy but ready to explore me. He starts at my shoulders and moves down to massage me. Panting, he asks me to play with him, and then he will do me. I pull him into me and put pressure on his ass. Slowly we grind on each other and come together. It doesn't happen often. "Thank God, I have missed this." I reach over and turn on the bedside light. He sits up and notices a portrait of my dad in an air force uniform; his WWII flying helmet sits beneath his picture. "Yes, the colonel was quite a man. Someday I'll tell you some stories about his WWII experience. He was a bomber pilot who dropped some 101st Airborne over Germany on D-Day and evacuated wounded in Italy, and I am very proud to be his daughter." Sam says, "Tell me more," and I tell him, "I need sleep. I am not yet fully healed."

Another gym session, and I decide to make tacos and have Dos Equis to drink. Maybe a movie tonight. Sam says, "Sounds good. I'd like to see *Das Boot*." Excellent film. Jurgen Prochnow is wonderful, and the tragic end will

bring tears to your eyes. No sexual interruptions during the film. We cuddle together, and I interpret some of the German to help him understand the dialogue between Captain and crew. I think we are both surprised how quickly we have become so comfortable with each other.

Sam is in the gym lifting heavy weights. His muscles quiver and flex as he forces the bar overhead. I admonish him because I couldn't possibly handle the weight as his spotter. "Don't worry. I can handle much more." He smacks my ass and says, "Come on. I'll change the weight and spot you." We then head for the cardio room for my benefit, such a gentleman, Sam.

A hot shower at home, and we settle into homemade tacos and beer. We play with each other, and I begin to feel a burning in my genitals—hot sauce from the tacos, not the best. I walk gingerly to the bathroom and wet a soapy washcloth. Relief. I return to the room and clean Sam's hands. "Okay, continue, Sam, and I will as well." All shyness gone, he pulls his erection to my mouth and says, "Love your mouth on me." Swiftly he bends me over and forcefully thrusts his cock until he releases the

K. A. ZARTMAN

pent-up energy. "I can't get enough of you, Purple." Sam has nicknamed me because of my hair. Sam frowns, and I ask, "What is troubling you?" "Just a sudden memory of a buddy killed in Nam." "Never kind, war does not discriminate. You are here, safe." A kiss, and we call it a night.

We are talking over dinner at the steakhouse, and Sam relates a few stories of his platoon in Nam. I lost several friends and could see the cost of war in the choppers we took care of in Texas. I reflect on how I felt in Hawaii watching the C130s land and discharge the black body bags and flag-covered coffins arriving daily, a seemingly endless supply. "Okay, enough sad; let's go home and make happy!" Now brave, Sam pushes me to the bedroom, rips our clothes off, and frantically takes me hard and strong. Gentle in the aftermath, he massages my breasts and kisses my scars. "Purple, I am so glad I met you." "Ditto, gunny. How 'bout another round?" Tenderly, he circles his fingers in me, and I casually slide my hand down and up on his erection. Feeling some jerks and quivers, I speed up my hand and pull his cock between my breasts. I am fascinated to watch the spurts of ejaculate

44

cover the scars on my chest. "Stay still, and I'll clean us up. Close your eyes, gunny. I want you to stay here tonight and spoon with you." The tactile feel of Sam is so different—hard, rippled muscles, heat, and the scent of sex and after-shave. "Sleep well and dream happy, Sam." I have developed strong feelings for this man. How does he feel?

We go out to a wonderful restaurant and have a generous meal of lamb, potatoes, salad, and red wine. We talk and squeeze shoulders, thighs, and take furtive detours to our groins. Ready for home, we head to the car. Stripping our clothes, I grip his erection and suck hard. He soon warns me he is going to come. He tries to pull me off him, and I say, "No, gun-ny, I want to taste you. Don't be afraid. Did you have girls in Nam?" "No. I was mostly in the country and had a platoon to watch over. Besides, we had contests in the field to see who could cum the fastest from their hands." I laugh. "Combat brothers!"

I am feeling stronger. The pig valve the sur-geons have inserted is healed, and I feel like taking a short hike. Sam surprises me, and we drive three hours to Moab, Utah. Scenic beauty around every curve: unworldly sentinel silent in the heat, nature's paintbrush to a masterpiece. Several bottles of water, and our legs are ready for a rest. Sam suggests we have lunch and book a hotel room rather than face a three-hour drive home. Our room has a wonderful view: tall, stately, red-rock pillar and white-capped river beneath them. We take a shower and flush the grime down the handsome pebbled drain in the shower. We dry off, turn the air-conditioner down, and collapse on the king-size bed. Sam massages my tired calves and thighs, arousing more than my leg muscles. His magic hands trail up to my sex and continue to massage me. Slipping into me and slowly pulling in and out as he trails kisses up my belly and captures a breast rolling the nipple with his tongue. I allow him to continue, and I begin to fondle his balls and ass. He presses his ass hard into my hands. "Wrap your legs around me and put your hands back on my ass. Force me hard into you." I turn my ankles to cup his ass a little firmer. Whispering to me, he says, "I think I love you." "Ditto, gunny." We are together. Patting my ass, he says, "Come on, Purple—I am starving." Delicious chicken salad sandwiches on sourdough bread and cold, sweet, peach tea. Could this day get any better?

We return to our room, and yeah, the day improves. We succumb to sleep and wake almost subconsciously beginning to have sex. "Sam, what does an orgasm feel like for a man?" "What do you mean?" "What do you feel before you come? Is it pain? Pressure? Cramping? What? I just want to know if it feels the same for men as women, though pleasurable for both. I feel the buildup of pressure and, when relief comes, the pulsing and warm wetness that follows." Sam is more introspective; it's like he feels "pressure, you know, like a sudden puncture of a tire and the release of air. All I know is it feels fantastic, just wish I could get hard again, immediately. It is the absolute proof of your manhood." "I've talked to guys paralyzed, and they would rather have the ability to cum over the ability to walk." "Christ, what a paradox men are."

We are back in the gym, and an errant young man swats my behind when I get up from a weight bench. Sam, the possessive marine, yells at him and threatens to flatten him if he doesn't back off. Secretly pleased with the attention, I pat Sam's shoulder and tell him I'm okay. After leaving, we stop and get turkey sandwiches and iced tea. "Let's watch a movie. We haven't seen one for a while." Studying my selection, he pulls *Tora, Tora, Tora*. it was the code word the Japanese used to signal home as the secret attack on Pearl Harbor. It is about the buildup to the attack from both Japanese and American perspectives. Quite different, the film has both American and Japanese producers and directors. The rigid formality of the Japanese is in stark contrast to the American fumbling attempt to discern a possible attack on the U.S. "If, when, where?" Sam peppers me with questions. I had no idea of the complications involved. December 7, 1941, a day that will live in infamy. Roosevelt's famous edict.

Calmed by the import of the film, we make gentle love, and Sam says, "We should get married." Shocked, I will have to consider carefully. I am seventy-one years old, and Sam is sixty-six. "What would the future hold for us?" We become anxious teenagers again and have fast, furious sex; the sweat blooms on both, and we are exhausted but satisfied. Sex, the best panacea for troubled minds. A few days pass, and we go to dinner. Sam presses me for an answer. I don't know. I'm fearful of future medical problems and other situations. Sam assures me we can handle anything together.

He stretches and asks me to tell him one of Dad's war stories. I think of a humorous one. Dad was flying a C47-Gooney Bird with medical supplies and injured soldiers. A sudden storm at altitude will force Dad to land. Faced with the dilemma, the copilot says there is a temporary landing strip only ten miles to the south. Dad turns, the plane drops 7,000 feet, and scans the windshield for evidence of a runway. Getting close, he sets his flaps, radios to the nurses in the hold to hang on—it could get rather bumpy. Saddened as the runway looms large in the view, Dad realizes it is made of special pallets that blow tires. Pulling back the throttle, he tries his best for a smooth landing, but the plane bumps, and everyone on board feels the strong jolt when a front tire blows. "Damn, what now?" Exiting the bird, Dad and his copilot notice another larger cargo plane at the end of the runway. They run to an open hatch, and a young sergeant appears when they call for help. "What can I do for you, Captain?"

Dad explains their situation and hopes he can borrow a tire. They have injured aboard and need to get airborne again. The sergeant smiles and says, "We blew a tire too on landing, but let's take a look and see if we can loan you one that will fit." Grabbing a toolbox, the three circle the plane and decide one will work if they can wrestle it off. He chuckles and says, "This is a general's plane, so back me up when you report in." Two hours on the ground, and Dad is ready to take off, after checking the status of the injured. Everyone is still okay, but please, no more delays. Sam smiles and says, "Only during wartime. Tell me another one."

I tell him the story of my uncle Bill, one of the original Darby's Rangers. He is taken prisoner in Germany and sent to a POW camp in Poland. He and a fellow prisoner escape with great difficulty and start a long trek to U.S. lines in Italy. They make their way south and luckily find a bombed-out home filled with food and a hoard of woman's underwear. Confiscating a baby stroller from the basement, they fill it with their treasures and sell underwear to women desperate to have some. Underwear is in great demand during wartime. "Can you imagine,

Sam?" Bill weighs only 110 pounds when he is found by the allies in Italy. "I love hearing your war stories, so profound and only known to veterans who lived through them." Sam hugs and kisses me. We need to talk about ourselves. Do I really want to marry again at my age? It does have some merit. We discuss where we will live, what my kids will think, and how will my health hold up.

"Enough talk. Suck on me, and then I will return the favor." I pull him to my mouth and suck hard for a long time until he stills and explodes in my mouth. Shyly, he says, "Now you. I have never done this, so you will need to guide me." "Relax, gunny; you will do well." I pull him down to me and tell him to lick and suck me. "Put your fingers in me while you are busy." I jerk and quiver from his actions and grab him to enter me. Hard, furious, we cum loudly, turn and grin at each other. Shit, sex is my all-time favorite activity.

CHAPTER 14

I CALL ALL three of my kids. The boys are positive: "Go for it, Mom!" My daughter, the psychiatrist, is initially negative but relents and says, "Come for a visit. I can't wait to meet him." The next few weeks we iron out some details. Sam will move in with me. My house is much larger; I have the art studio, library, three bedrooms, and two baths, furnished completely. Sam will bring a chest of drawers, books and tools, a sad lot for sixty years of living. I will buy a new chest for Sam; his 1980s oak furniture is not to my taste. I will make room and clear some shelves in the library for his books. We consider our financial outlook. My home is paid for. I collect Social Security, Medicare (thank God).

Sam has some savings, Social Security, and his medical is covered by the VA. I look forward to my second retirement and life with a partner.

I am running late for the gym. I don't see Sam after searching the gym. I go to the front counter and ask Paul if he has seen Sam. "Come with me to the office. Sit down and I must tell you what happened." Immediately nervous, I follow him. "Sam was here, and he had a heart attack, dropped the weight bar on his chest. We called an ambulance, and they took him to the VA."

Thanking Paul, I rush out and drive to the VA hospital emergency room. "Are you family?" "No, but I will be. How is he? Can I see him?" "Sam has had a heart attack and has severe bruising from a weight bar. He is stable and having some needed tests." They will tell me when I can see him. After several hours of intense worry and what-ifs, a nurse motions for me to follow her. "Hey, Purple! I'm still here." I smile and tell him, "Looks like you will have to lower the weight bars to mine." So challenging to be old. I pat his hand with the IV taped to it. I talk to the doctor, and he tells me Sam will be here about a week; they will put three stents in his heart and start medications. "Gunny, you got off easy." I see Sam every day and tell him he can just move in with me. "I'm so glad you're mine, and I can't wait to get home."

Flexing his hips, he winks at me. I smile and tell him, "When the time comes." A week goes by, and we stop at Sam's to pick up clothes, tooth-brush, and toiletries. Home at last, soup, grilled cheese, and I tuck Sam in blankets on the sofa and put in *The Enemy Below*, a '50s sub movie he will enjoy. Before long, Sam is asleep and breathing softly. I kiss his forehead and start the laundry. Laundry is done, and I check on Sam. He winks and says, "Bed."

I help him to the bedroom and put on elas-tic-waist pajama pants. Smoothing my hands over his belly, he wants to spoon with me. I lie down beside him, and wincing, he pulls me to him and plays with my breasts. I kiss him and say, "Sleep, sleep, sweet Sam."

CHAPTER 15

MY WEEK IS busy as it is the final week to clean up any loose ends at work. No early mornings, no late nights, time for painting and Sam. I call the kids and workout a timetable to visit. I take Sam to his checkup, and he is pronounced good, okay for sex, just nothing too harsh. I will be the judge. I pick up two chicken salads on the way home, no interruptions at home. Tucking him into bed, he reaches for me, and I lower his sweatpants and tell him to warn me if he has any pain. I gently fondle his cock, and soon he is groaning. I strip and lower myself onto him. We make gentle love. I kiss him and say, "Lunch."

We have lunch, and I tell Sam he needs a nap. Stubborn, he resists but closes his eyes and is soon asleep. "I need a shower; will you help me?" I start the water and tell Sam to lean against the wall. I will clean him and remove the tape residue left over from the hospital. As I soap him, the tape marks disappear, and a hard erection beckons me to help. Again, I remind Sam to tell me if he has pain. "The only pain I have is in my cock." "I have just the right medication for that. Turn around, and I will give it to you." Sam is passionate and comes loudly. "Home, sweet home, gunny." Sam is flushed, so I say, "Come lie down. I want to take your blood pressure." I retrieve my blood pressure module and place the cuff on Sam. I watch the digital readout and relax when it reads 132/81. Sam is okay.

We gradually increase our sexual activity and go to the gym for light workouts. Life is good again! Now to make it better. I strip off my clothes and lower Sam's sweatpants, pleased with his erection. I pull him to my mouth, and he plays with me. Groaning, I bend over and guide him into me. Aggressively, he takes me and collapses against me. "God, Purple, what you do to me." We relax a bit and go to the living room. I open a bottle of wine and collect several photo books from the library. Sam looks with interest at the hundreds of photos from around the world and of family members now dead. I turn a page and break into tears. "What is it, baby?" "It is my little sister, Linda, holding my granddaughter." Linda is dead; she committed suicide in June. I explain how this tragedy came about.

Linda had severe multiple sclerosis for twenty years. She fell, and a trip to the hospital shows damage and an open wound to an ankle. Not able to walk or stand, she is sent to an assisted living facility nearby. She refuses food and drink; I think because she knows she would not be able to be independent again in her home. The cycle of refusing food and drink continues for a month. We notice the changes in her and encourage her to have something. Her breathing changes, blood pressure drops, and we know she is failing. Suicide by starvation; so tormenting, but what can we do? She refuses a stomach tube and waits to die. This strong, independent woman, a deep-underground miner, a parole officer at Buena Vista Prison, she gave up. Linda died on the fifth of June, no husband, no kids, a houseful of unopened Amazon boxes. So tragic. "Thank God I have you, Sam—a year of unexpected events, and you are the best of them." Sam hugs me and comforts me; the tears disappear, and life continues.

Our burgers are on the grill, beans are in the oven, and beer is on ice. We cuddle in a chaise and talk about the future. Kissing and fondling each other, we drift off to sleep and wake with a large moon lighting the back-yard. Sam says, "Your hair is the color of the ring around the moon. A lavender moon, and my life partner's body next to me. A glorious night." "Come in, and we can celebrate!" Sam pulls me up, and we walk hand in hand to the house. Our hands are all over each other, and we make frantic love; talking in the aftermath, I tell Sam I want to take him to Washington, DC, to visit my grandfather's grave in Arlington, see JFK's, and show him the Vietnam memorial. Sam is delighted, and I phone for reservations. We will stay in a luxury hotel close to every-thing, and Sam wants to know what to pack. Comfortable clothes and shoes.

CHAPTER 16

AFTER LANDING IN DC, we take a taxi to the hotel. We take in the sumptuous lobby and are shown to our room. Beautiful, rich wood furniture, Persian rugs, and a huge bath, stocked bar. The room is too traditional in design for me. I like contemporary, neutral colors, and clean lines. Sam agrees: "Reminds me of a Grandma's house." I start a bath with the scented oil provided and call Sam to join me. Sam pulls me to him and plays with my breasts; trailing south, he massages me and then spins me around to massage him in turn. Now facing each other, Sam pulls me onto him, and we create splashing water over the sides of the massive tub.

Clean and dry, we dress for dinner and take the elevator to a crowded dining room: white tablecloths, candles, muted lighting from the chandeliers, and a white-coated waiter to take our order of salmon dinners. We have enjoyed our meal and return to the room after asking for a 7:00 a.m. wakeup call. It will be a long, challenging day tomorrow. Waking, we dress and decide to have a breakfast of eggs, sausage, and pancakes and strong coffee. Fortified, we call for a taxi to take us to Arlington National Cemetery. I know where Grandpa is buried, so we slowly walk the landscaped paths until we come to the section and row number. There seems to be more neat rows growing white crosses. We find Grandpa, and I stand in silence, remembering his full head of white hair and bouncing on his knee. Sam takes my hand, and we wander through the many visitors to the JFK torch-lit grave. Kennedy, a favorite of mine, is silent, with a profound crowd gazing at the president's last residence. I ask Sam if he ever saw *PT109*, a film of Kennedy and crews awaiting rescue in the South Pacific. No, Sam has not seen the film, and I tell him I have the DVD; we can watch it at home.

A brisk and crowded walk later, we arrive at the Vietnam memorial. Sam is hesitant, looking at the enormous, black, stone monolith holding some 57,000 names of the dead. I put my arms around Sam as he stops periodically and leans his head against the cool, hard surface. We come to the end of this tearful journey, and Sam turns to look one last time. He bursts into tears. "God, the cost of war. The thousands of wounded are not memorialized but remembered for their loss as well." Sam shakes his head. "Not worth the cost." "It's over, Gunny; let your memories guide you, not the silences of the dead." We grip hands and return to the hotel. A quick dinner, and Sam is aggressive in the elevator to our room. Opening the door, he forces me to the bed, rips off his clothes and mine, and violently takes me, venting his anger and soothing his soul. "Sorry, baby, that wall got me all worked up." "I understand. It is easy to see the artist's vision of what the memorial was built for." "It grips everybody...those who fought and those at home." "A sad thing, did you notice? Most of the people were older, not many young." "The young were not yet born when the war ended." "Purple, you have such compassion, not pity. I love you." Sam is quiet and slowly rubs my fingers on the flight home. "Thank you for taking me. I needed a reminder of the past to push me to the future."

"When we get home, I want to show you

pictures of mine." When we get home, we have a quiet dinner and a glass of wine. I lead him to the sofa and retrieve several discs from the library. "Are we watching a film?" "No, Sam, these discs were made by my sister-in-law. She took all the slides Dad took over the years and put them together with music. Germany, Austria, Italy, Israel, Turkey, Egypt, and all the Scandinavian countries." Sam is animated as we see the Wailing Wall and churches in Jerusalem and the monuments of Copenhagen, the Eiffel Tower in France, and numerous photos of Armed Forces Day in the U.S. The disc finishes, and the last classical piano music ends. "I'll put in another disc. It is Iceland. We were there for three years; it was still a communist country while we were there. No trees, racks of drying fish, and a visit to Whale Bay where a recently legally caught whale was being cut up and passed through a steaming hole to break down the blubber." Fascinated, Sam says, "You have seen so much of the world." "Yes, I have, so lucky to have such wonderful parents and the opportunities to see other cultures, lands, and the lives they have." I insert another disc, and Sam leans forward with interest. "You will love the music on this one. It is on Gettysburg; we had a family home Dad built there close to the battlefield." I name a few of the monuments standing on the grounds of the famous battles Little Round Top and Pickett's Charge. If my memory serves, there were 50,000-some brave souls dead and thousands more injured in just a matter of days. "Can you imagine, Sam, about the same numbers as Nam in days rather than years. Simple, single-shot rifles, swords, and cannon fire, no aircraft, AK47s, no mortars, just the same patriots fighting for a cause." "Right or wrong, war is not judged by the participants but those who come after." Sam kisses me and murmurs, "Profound, so profound." I turn the lights off, lock the front door, and lead Sam to the bedroom.

Frantic to couple, Sam pounds away and suddenly pulls out and slumps on my chest. I feel wetness and ask Sam, "What's wrong?" he sits up, wipes his eyes gruffly on the sheet, and says, "God, I hate reminders of war. I can hear the mortars and smell the stench of a stomach wound to a buddy." I kiss him and pull him to my chest, stroking his back. He falls asleep, comforted by my hands. When we wake, last night's memories shield Sam.

He says, "Let's go to Glenwood Springs and take the gondola to the top."

CHAPTER 17

WE ARRIVE TOO early for the gondola, so we have hearty breakfast at a mom-and-pop café, simple food, cooked well, and a slice of homemade apple strudel. Yes, it's going to be a good day. The gondola opens, and we are lone passengers to the top. We notice the leaves of aspens have already turned red and gold, a harbinger of fall, and the cool winds confirm it. The cave-and-caverns tour reveal massive fissures filled with stalactites and dripping water. Ancient sentinels remain silent in the gloom, and we are getting cold. The uphill climb and stairs plus the altitude has both of us with labored breathing. *Remember, you are old, slow and easy.* We take the mountain coaster ride after a brief rest to enjoy the fall sunshine and climb back into the gondola, now crowded with noisy families.

We head home and take a detour of the

Grand Mesa, peppered with green pines, blue spruce, and fields of the red-and-orange aspens greeting the season. Coming back down, we pull over to see the raging Colorado River, absent any rafters, but pause to enjoy the scent of pine and clear, cold water rushing south. Such as beautiful state. I hope its inhabitants will maintain it for the future. Sam hugs me, and we return to his pickup.

Home again, and we collapse on the bed, naptime. I wake when I feel Sam massaging my calves and thighs. He is so good with his hands. He retrieves some massage oil and continues to knead the tight muscles. The massage oil helps to deaden the roughness of his hands. Slowly, he continues, bypassing my sex, and firmly kneads my breasts and shoulders. Suddenly, he stops and rubs the same area again and again. "What is that? I feel something funny in you." "Relax Sam, those are the wires the surgeon put in to close the breast. Sometimes you can feel them. Remember how the alarms went off at the airport?" He kisses my scars and then continues to spread the oil down my belly and lower. He twirls his fingers in me, and I smear my hands with oil form my chest and grip him tightly. "Squeeze harder, baby, and make me come." I follow the sergeant's orders and soon feel the jerks as he comes loudly. Geriatric sex, I recommend it.

CHAPTER **18**

WE ARE HAVING breakfast at a Village Inn across the street from the VA Hospital. A sign in the front of the hospital flashes a message to traffic: "The cost of freedom can be seen here." I wonder how many of the cars holding college students listening to the pulsing bass music and passing the sign will even read the message or understand it. I get so maudlin sometimes. I turn to Sam, and he looks a little pale, his breathing labored. I squeeze his thigh, and he smiles. "I'm fine." We stand, and Sam wobbles on his feet, clutching his chest; he moans and starts to collapse. I ask a nearby waiter to help me get him to the car—he is having a heart attack. "Should I call an ambulance?" I yell, "No, I'll take him to the VA across the street. I t will be much faster."

Braving the traffic in the busy street, I gun the car across traffic and blaring horns; the brakes squeal as I pull up to the emergency room. As I blow the horn, a few orderlies come out the automatic doors and put Sam on a gurney. He looks at me in pain and squeezes out, "I'm sorry." I follow them into a trauma room, and I am distracted by a grief nurse asking questions. I ignore her and yell, "Get a doctor in here now!" Sam is in frantic pain, and they are trying to get an IV in him. I hold his hand, and he relaxes for a moment to allow the nurse access for an IV. A doctor rushes in, and I read his name tag, Dr. Williams, orthopedics. I tell him we need a cardiac doctor, and he says, "I'm all that is available now." Sam is hooked up to monitors, and I watch the numbers fluctuate up and down. "Purple, where are you?" "I am right here, Sam—don't leave me."

It is foolish to believe a dying person can change his destiny by someone talking to them. I concentrate on the monitor and see the numbers sinking lower and lower. The doctor orders several drugs to be given and waits for a change to the monitor. Sam is now writhing on the gurney and not able to talk. The monitor soon slows and slows to a flat line, no pulse. I have lost Sam. They call a code, and a team races in

69

with a defib cart. Three jolts, I don't remember the number of joules, and they note the time of death. No pulse, no heartbeat, my Sam is gone.

Stunned, I go to the car and sit and cry for hours. It is dark when I turn the engine over and drive slowly home. Sam, Sam, you are gone, and I'm alone again. I grab his pillow and cry; it is so unfair. Haven't I been through enough this year?

I don't sleep. I get up and make some coffee at 3:00 a.m. I notice Sam's cup on the counter, and I savagely throw it at the wall in the kitchen. "Oh, Sam, why did you have to go?" I am empty. Three days have passed, and I cannot stop the tears or anger. I waited seventy years and then found my life mate only to have him taken from me. No more lavender moons, Sam; only blood-red lights the night.

CHAPTER **19**

I AM LYING in bed after a hot bath and two Tylenol PM tablets, hoping sleep will come. Glancing at the clock, I see it has been two hours, and my mind is still restless. Sam, no longer beside me; I cannot push myself to his body. I miss the warmth and feel of his erection against me. I roll over and pull my knees up. My hand seeks comfort between my legs, and still my mind drifts. Why was he taken from me? I have given my life over in care of others. I don't understand. Seventy years to find him; one day to lose him. Why, why, why? I cannot alter time or circumstance; no magician can bring him back to me. Accept what has happened and move forward.

I somewhat fear the future with no one beside me, but I have conquered fear before. The mind can banish thoughts and pain as quickly as the memory unfolds. The stroke has buried many early memories. I allow my thoughts to drift and face the fear of past events.

I am babysitting the neighbor's kids in Iceland. The captain and his wife are out to dinner at the officer's club. It is bitter cold, and the wind is shaking the aluminum walls of the Quonset hut home. The captain stumbles into the room and pulls me off the sofa. "What are you doing?" He jerks the blanket from me and pulls up my sweatshirt. I am panicked, twelve years old, and innocent to drunken behavior. I struggle to get out of his hands, but he is much stronger. "You will give me what I want. I want you." "Leave me alone," I shout. One of the kids wakes up and tempers his mood somewhat. My fear dissipates, and I run to the door, my escape. He grabs my hair, a pony-tail, and forces his tongue in my mouth. I bite down hard; he swears and smacks me. I kick him and warn him not to touch me. "My dad outranks you!" I yell and leave him shocked, standing in front of the open door. "Ugh, drunken grown-ups."

Another memory floats up and the fear returns. I am water-skiing to Ship Island. It is some miles out in the Gulf of Mexico. I cross a wake and clip the side of a channel buoy. I fall and swim to the buoy. Something brushes my thigh, and I try to get higher on the buoy. Dad has not noticed I have fallen, and my sibling spotter has not either. I anxiously scan the water for a fin; tiger sharks are known for these waters. I see a dark shape circling the buoy and hold my breath, waving an arm to alert Dad. A fin breaks the surface, and I scream. Moments later, the shadow jolts out of the water, and I recognize the bottlenose dolphin, not a shark.

The memories float to the top and seem to be in chronological order. I am in the navy and serving as a crewmember on a Ps2 prop plane. A junior pilot fresh from jet school in Jacksonville, Florida, is at the controls as we descend to the airfield in Corpus Christi. His inexperience is evident in the swaying of the aircraft. The senior pilot reminds him of the sensitive brakes: "Do not stand on them when you feel the bite of the tires on the field." I pull my Mae West closer and check for loose connections. The field of vision ahead bounces and veers to the side. The rear tires contact the field, and our airspeed is too fast. Junior stands on the brakes while the senior yells to release the pressure on the brakes. The fire ignition light draws my attention and fuels my pounding heart. The sights and sounds of a wailing fire truck speeding beside us, and I calm my thumping heart. I scramble out of my seat and the constraints holding me to it; my Mae West and parachute make it difficult to exit the side hatch and the prop rotors are still spinning. The junior pilot rises and vomits all over the back of his seat. Pride of the navy, he will learn quickly in Nam.

I dismiss several memories of James in drunken ardor and then remember a fire. I am home from college classes and pick up the boys from the sitter. They consume a snack and go upstairs to play. I open a mathematics book and concentrate on finding puzzling answers. My oldest rushes into the room and says, "Come upstairs now." I run up the stairs and can smell smoke. I see it seeping under the kid's bedroom door. Checking the warmth of the door, I cautiously open it and see the flames swallowing the mattress, sheets, and comforter. Both boys are observing the flames from the hallway. I run to the upstairs bath, toss the contents of a wastebasket on the floor, and turn the bathtub faucet on full. It takes an eternity to fill the wastebasket, and it is heavy when I jerk it out and throw the contents on the mattress. I run to the master and scream at the 9-1-1 operator to send a fire truck. Returning to the room, I see the drapes have now caught fire, and I go to refill the waste can. My oldest is crying in the hallway, and I tell him to go open the front door for the fireman. "I'm sorry, I'm sorry, I'm sorry." I jerk the drapes down and throw more water on the smoking mattress. It is a king size, too heavy for me to lift. The fire-fighters race up the stairs, break the window, and saturate the mattress, drapes, and bedding before bending the soggy mess out of the second-story window. My heart stops pounding, and I call to the boys to come upstairs. There are orange tracks for Hot Wheels everywhere. "How did this start?" The older one, crying and in a halted voice, says, "I lost my Batman Hot Wheels. It rolled under the bed, and I couldn't find it, so I went into your room, and I couldn't find the flashlight, so I took Dad's lighter, so I could see under the bed. It scared me when the under caught fire." I squeeze him and say, "You should have come to me. It was an accident;

don't worry—Dad will understand." Ha! Fat chance! He will take it out on all of us.

It is midsummer, the temperatures are in the nineties, and the boys have begged for a pool. I purchase a small inflatable and fill it on the back patio for the boys to enjoy. It is Saturday—no classes, and James is at the airfield. The pool is filled, and water trickles over the sides; about a half hour later, the boys come in and open the patio screen door. They run from the kitchen through the door and jump into the pool. I warn them to be careful and not slip. I hear some clanking and look out the kitchen window; nothing seems amiss, so I go back to the dishes in the sink. My youngest, Tony, runs full speed toward the pool, and I hear him scream. The water in the pool has a red current running over the edges. My oldest has put a five-gallon glass Sparkle's water bottle in the pool. When Tony ran and jumped in, the bottle broke and cut Tony's legs. I lift Tony from the water and see his artery is pumping blood over my jeans. I carry him to the kitchen and sit him on the counter, blood pouring from numerous cuts and his artery. I pull a stack of kitchen towels and wrap them tightly around his legs. I grab my keys and rush to the car, driving him to the emergency room, my heart thumping like his artery. I keep pressure on the leg and ty to calm us. I am driving like a maniac and jerk to a stop at the hospital. The staff rushes us into a room and pulls the sodden towels from his legs. The plume of blood startles the attending, and he immediately applies pressure again. Tony is wheeled upstairs and returns two hours later covered with tiny black stiches and bleeding bandages. It is no wonder why in my later years I require open-heart surgery.

Kids, how quickly they can get into trouble. Adults too, but much worse because we should know the consequences. Spiraling forward my next memory, a painful one. I wake to the telephone ringing. It is 3:00 a.m. This can't be good. "This is Miss Lloyd. I'm a nurse at Kaiser Hospital. We have your son, Tony, here in the emergency room. We need you to come right away. His heart stopped several times, and we have used the defibrillator several times." I bolt from bed and race to the hospital. Tony is sleeping and has many tubes and hoses attached to him. I sit in an uncomfortable chair and watch the blips and beeps of the heart and lungs. It is now 8:00 in the morning. Tony wakes up groggy and sees me. I kiss him and hug him. What happened? He feels terrible. I explain his heart stopped, and they had to revive him several times. I ask what happened. He says, "I bought some LSD from a buddy, and I sat on a bus bench when I started feeling bad. Then I woke up here." "God, Tony! You almost died. The doctor told me the blood tests revealed arsenic in your system. The LSD was laced with poison." Someone is watching over this family. *Keep watching—we will try not to give you cause.*

I am at the furniture store helping a customer decide on new furniture for the living room. She has already chosen a navy-blue sofa with white contrast welts, very nice and in stock. She wants to see some end tables next to it. I move several, so she can see how they look. The last table is heavier than the others. I place it by the sofa. As I release the weight of the table, I feel a suction pinch in my lower back. I know something has let loose, but I'm able to function. I start having shooting pain in my back and down my right leg. I head home after making an appointment with my doctor and initiate a worker's comp claim. The next morning, after a painful night, I swing my legs to get out of bed and I'm struck by excruciating pain. I cannot stand, so I crawl slowly to the bathroom. My bladder is full. I cannot get up to the toilet, so I pee on the floor and breathe heavily. I cannot stand or move without strong pain. The fear comes as I think about a future paralyzed or in constant pain. One of the warehouse men comes and gets me to go see the doctor. I cannot walk, so I stand and then sit down on the stairs and slowly make my way down to the van. I learn that if I have support against a wall or a person, I can scoot sideways to a table or chair, which I can't sit in. The doctor pokes and prods and orders an MRI. Two discs will have to be removed and some muscle which holds the back in place. I'm in for a long haul. Surgery is scheduled, and I return home for two weeks of intense pain and must rely on the kids for laundry, cooking, and shopping. The fear grows as the doctor explains possible complications and what-ifs. I listen but disregard his warnings. I just want the intense pain to go away. I have the surgery. A week in the hospital, and I can go home. I can stand with help, the pain is more moderate, but I'm unable to sleep unless I'm in a recliner propped with pillows. I could easily get addicted to opiates, but I watch my intake of pills. The kids have been a big help, and I'm relieved when the first worker's comp check arrives. After three months of painful rehab, I can return to work, no lifting and platitudes from the surgeons. I will never be the same. Learn to live with it. Yeah, I know the drill. Thankful I can walk, it is many years later, despite minor fears along the way, before intense fear returns to me.

I am having a stroke. I wait for something to happen. I expect something to dull the sensations I am feeling, but the inability to walk or move has been paralyzed. I have fallen three times trying to get to the living room sofa and a phone. I struggle to turn or move, so I can get off my arm and shoulder, now painful from falling. My brain is mush, and I cannot get my limbs to obey. If I could get to the phone, I would call 9-1-1, though I know I'm unable to talk. I lie still and try to absorb the sensations, hoping to get to the sofa. I worry that as the stroke strengthens, I will never wake to normal. I spend the night on the floor, and when I wake with a severe headaches and wobble to the bathroom, I must hold on to something for support. I drive myself to the doctor, who immediately sends me to the hospital. An MRI and brain scan show a massive stroke and unusual cardiac activity. I spend the night at the hospital, and several cardiologists visit and listen to my heart. Unusual sounds and rhythms cause a stir, and several more are allowed in the room to learn new sounds. I am a lab experiment but grateful for the attention.

The next morning several doctors arrive and explain what has happened and that I need open-heart surgery and a valve replaced, and a very large aneurism needs to be repaired. I could die at any moment. Fear grips me, and I ponder the challenges ahead. Surgery is scheduled, and I have made arrangements to be off work for the grueling months ahead. More what-ifs, but at seventy, who knows? I have been through so much. Can my body hold up for a few more years? Fear, the great leveler through life. How you handle it and become immune to the pull of the unknown determines your future.

I roll over. It is 4:00 a.m., and my brain

wants to sleep now after painful memories recede and disappear. Can I sleep now and perhaps rest this tired body? God, Sam, I want you here again. I am so frustrated that sleep eludes me, and light is seeping through the sheers. Will I see Sam again? No, it's just fanciful thinking. I am in the Darwin camp. When you die, you are gone, no heaven, no hell, just gone from life. If the priests are right, he is looking down at me and extending a hand to join him. No, that's bullshit! How can so many believe in the afterlife? Use your brain; there is none. Profound thoughts continue to rattle my brain. I lean to science and ask sleep to come. I am alone and shall remain so until my time comes. I contemplate if I should jump-start the end. I vault out of bed and locate the bottle of oxycodone. I take two and wonder if the remaining twenty-eight pills are enough to kill me. Don't! I'm not ready to leave. Images of my kids and grandkids still my hand. I am stronger than the pull of heartache that draws tears. Enough, enough. I let the pills lull me to sleep. Accept life as it is and perhaps the lavender moon will shine again and light my spirit. My eyes close and sleep befriends me once again.